Malkia

Short Stories

Malkia
Short Stories

WANJIRU KIMANI

INK Books LLC
McDonough, Georgia

Published by INK Books LLC
McDonough, Georgia

Scripture is taken from The King James Version (KJV)
of the Bible.

Cover and Story Illustrations: Jeffrey Onyango

Please contact INK Books LLC for bulk purchases at
inkbooks16@gmail.com or (470) 289-6299.

Printed in the United States of America: May 2020

ISBN: 978-1-7347164-0-5 (Paperback)

Dedicated to my daughter Njeri and all other Malkias (Queens), young and old.

Acknowledgements

I thank God, the giver of all wonderful gifts.

Kimani, my loving husband, I appreciate you.
Kung'u and Njeri, the fruits of my womb, I
thank you.

I am grateful for the gift of a loving and
supportive family. Njeri, my loving mums, I
can't thank you enough. My brothers and
sisters, thank you.

Dr. Wachanga, Mr. Collins, and Ms. Green,
thank you for your precious time.

Table of Contents

Poem: Malkia (Queen)

May the sound of the drums that seemed so far and
distant,
Oh Malkia
beat louder and louder and awaken your sleepy soul.

May your hips that seemed so stiff,
Oh Malkia
slowly and gradually sway to the beat.

May your feet that seemed immobile,
Oh Malkia
stamp and move, as your soul is inflamed by the
rhythm.

Free your soul,
Oh Malkia
Come alive to the African beat.

Shine, Malkia, shine
as you radiate the unity of many colors
You, Malkia
The center that unites many colors
Turning them black and powerful and beautiful

Arise
Malkia of the Most High God!

Arise and dance, Malkia
Dance to the African beat.

The Child Within

"Arghhhh," Rita murmured in frustration as she hurriedly made a left into W 34th Street. She wiped the grease from her face. The smudge was made by the coconut oil melting from her puff afro. She was uneasily aware that she smelled like Indian curry, a smell that clung to her body and clothes since she first started her waitressing job. She tried to mask it with her Victoria's Secret Sweet Pea Body Mist, but it was hopeless.

From the side pocket of her tote bag, she took a pair of brown wooden earrings and put them on, then adjusted her green flowery African scarf around her neck. Finally, she checked to see if her one-page portfolio was still in her bag. Satisfied, she hurriedly walked toward 5th avenue. She was running late for her 3.30pm appointment, thanks to Ahmed, the son of the man who owned Raja's Indian Cuisine. She had asked him to let her leave 30 minutes before her shift ended, but customers kept streaming in and he just wouldn't let her off. Worse, the restaurant was two servers short on that day.

Rita had to attend to two stations. As she worked, she was anxiously aware that Ahmed was only playing poker on his computer, but pretended to be balancing the books. All the while Rita labored, she looked at her watch every few minutes. When she was ready to leave, Ahmed said she had to serve her full shift and that, if she did not like his instructions, she was free to look for another job.

"Ahmed could be selfish and lazy sometimes," she thought. In fact, she had never seen such a lazy man in her entire life. All the men in her life worked hard for their families. Her father worked from sunrise to sunset, and never complained. She watched him till his land, and his hard work and sweat always brought great returns. He taught her that in due time hard work always pays off.

Whenever Ahmed felt like leaving work, he simply left, which she considered completely unethical. Each day at 3pm, Ahmed marched out of the restaurant and was seen heading to the neighboring gas station to watch recaps of past cricket games with his friend Rashid. Why couldn't he work his full shift like her? He was nothing like his father, who worked hard, and who treated his employees with honor and respect. He recently told her that if she continued with her hard work, he would promote her to head waitress. He reminded her so much of her father.

Sadly, his father came to the restaurant 2, or at

most, 3 days a week. The rest of the days Ahmed was in charge. He never seemed to care that the restaurant was frequently under-staffed or that the place was swarming with grumbling clients at the busy lunch hour and anyone who dared to question him would reckon with his ruthlessness. He was reputed for firing both servers and chefs with no notice. Faced with the grim prospects of being jobless, Rita had no choice but to stay on until 3pm.

She made a right turn into 5th avenue and could see the Bleep Modeling Agency building a block away. It was impossible to miss it. The agency had a huge colorful billboard of female models wearing bright-colored swimming costumes, holding surfing boards. Already, a group of women had lined up outside. Rita stopped and took a deep breath. Her heart started racing. Her dream was about to begin.

"Hi, is this the line for the Sizzling Summer Models audition?" she asked the last girl in the queue. The girl was stunningly beautiful. When Rita spoke, the young woman looked down, as if she did not hear

She made a right turn into 5th avenue and could see the Bleep Modelling Agency building a block away

the question. It turned into an awkward moment. Rita didn't know whether she should repeat her question, or ignore her and continue as if nothing had happened. Then the lady pulled out her mirror from her gold shoulder bag.

"Yes, this is it. The line is hardly moving," said the girl as she looked at her mirror. She stopped to apply yet another coat of a flashy-red glossy lipstick.

The aspiring model had ivory skin, long false eyelashes, a blonde wig, and she wore large green earrings.

She wore a tight red leather mini-skirt, 4-inch red heels, and a flowery green shirt.

"Thanks," Rita said, stopping behind her, and observing the rest of the young women. They came from diverse races and sported unique hairstyles, clothes and makeup, and even though they had different physical characteristic, all were painfully skinny. All along, Rita had assumed that there would only be a few models auditioning. However, she lost heart to realize the competition would be intense.

"I'm Anne-Marie Stephens," the blonde girl said, looking Rita over.

"Pleasure, Anne-Marie," responded Rita. "My name is Rita."

Since coming to America the year before, Rita noted that Americans had trouble pronouncing African names. They especially had problems pronouncing her last name, Cheptoo, which in her Kalenjin language, meant "born when visitors are around."

One American had mis-pronounced her name as "Chipped-toe" and then looked at Rita's feet as if to confirm it all. To save time and avoid complications, she now introduced herself simply as "Rita."

"You have a cute accent," Anne-Marie said. "Where are you from?"

In Rita's experience, that question was inevitable.

She was never certain if people asked about her nationality out of curiosity, or simply to make small talk. Whatever their motive, she felt intruded upon. Back home in Africa, people didn't ask so many questions. Here, everyone was way too nosy.

"I'm from Kenya."

"You're far from home! How do you like it here?"

"I love it!"

That was the wisest answer. Anything else and she might arouse suspicion.

Annie-Marie talked non-stop. She was intent on digging even deeper: "I have a friend in Alabama who was dating an African man," she said. "I think this guy was Kenyan, but I'm not quite sure. Every morning he would go for a five-mile run, and never broke a sweat. Boy! You Kenyans run those long-distance races with such ease. Do you run?"

"No, I don't," Rita replied.

Already, she was getting sick and tired of all the questioning. Why did she pick a talk with this prying girl?

"Oh well. I'm originally from Alabama. I have only been in New York for eight months. I have been modeling for years. What about you? Did you model back in Kenya?"

"Yes, I did," Rita lied.

The only modeling she had done was once in high school—in a friendly modeling show hastily thrown together by her peers.

"When are you going back to Kenya?"

Rita could not take it anymore. She excused herself, explaining that she needed to make a quick phone call to her roommate, Abi. She took out her cell phone and dialed a number. It went straight to voicemail, so she decided to write a quick text message.

Abi was short for Abisola. She was originally from Nigeria but had lived in America now for over five years. Knowledgeable, it was she who had informed Rita about the Bleep Modeling Agency interview. She also helped Rita put together a résumé.

"My sista-ohhh!" Abisola exclaimed when she saw Rita's résumé for the first time. "You better learn how to lie if you are to survive here in America."

By the time Abi was done "beautifying" the résumé, Rita could hardly recognize the details in the "work and experiences" section. Of course, Abi was clever. Under "References" she provided her uncle's number. Apparently, Rita had vast experience modeling at this person's agency.

In truth, Abi's uncle owned a little temporary stall for African clothes near Chinatown. She had assured Rita that if the people at Bleep called her uncle's number, he would talk her up as instructed. Realizing that she stood better chances if she agreed, she went along.

For as long as she could remember, Rita had wanted to become a model. She was born in Elgeyo Marakwet in North-Western Kenya and hailed from the Kalenjin tribe. Her modeling dream started when Miss Kenya visited her village on missionary work. Rita was impressed that the visiting model had won the Miss Kenya title a few months prior to her visit. She was about six feet tall, and her skin complexion was ebony.

Rita vividly remembered what the visiting model had worn: a pair of blue, skinny jeans and a pink T-shirt. She sported her crown and clad in a colorful sash, which bore the following colorful emblazonment: "Miss Kenya."

Mesmerized, Rita and the other village girls sat down on the dirt surrounding the angelic model. Miss Kenya was the most beautiful woman Rita had laid her eyes on, the true definition of a Nubian queen. She told the girls stories of the numerous places she had visited, and the famous people she met. She seemed especially fond of New York and called it the modeling capital city.

The model even joined the girls in a game of Kati, a children's game that was similar to Dodgeball. All you needed to do was avoid getting hit by a small plastic ball, and if you were hit, you joined the growing group of ousted players sitting on the side, waiting for the round to end , for them to try yet again until the last player standing.

Afterwards, everyone, including the visitor, held hands and formed a circle to sing Swahili children's songs. Rita remembered how, the moment they were

Miss Kenya was the most beautiful woman Rita had laid her eyes on, the true definition of a Nubian queen.

asked to make the circle, she elbowed her way through the crowd of village girls, scrambling to hold the model's hand. It all felt wonderful just to touch her.

It was that particular Miss Kenya visit that lit the fire in Rita. Since then, she just could not extinguish her desire to become a model. Rita's father dismissed her ideas as a childhood fantasy. In spite of his discouraging words, he caught her modeling before her peers. As she strutted the imaginary catwalk, Rita swayed her hips, her long neck held straight up, feeling like a million dollars throughout. When the behavior did not stop, her father asked Rita's mother to talk her out of it.

When it became clear that Rita would not be quitting, her mother whispered in her ear, "Just be careful not to do it in your father's presence." And that became their little pact.

Rita's mother was one of the few nurses in her village. She once told Rita that, during her youth, she dreamt of becoming an airhostess. Her desire was to travel to different countries and see the world, but she had to face reality when her applications were all rejected. All the rejections, she said, were probably a sign that this path wasn't meant for her.

After high school, Rita found out that a college in New York was giving nursing scholarships to girls from her district who had done excelled in their final exams. She performed exceptionally well, so she applied with her father's help. The man was finally excited that his daughter had chosen the *right* path. He was even happy to pay the exorbitant application fee.

Almost five months later, Rita's admission letter came. She was one of the lucky girls picked. Quietly, she knew this would be her gateway to her lifelong dream—modeling, in the modeling capital of the world!

As they escorted her to Jomo Kenyatta International Airport in Nairobi, her father looked at Rita and said, "I know you will make me proud. Nursing is a great career. Remember all we have taught you. Work hard and be wise."

Rita nodded in agreement.

With each passing minute, the line to the modeling interviews got longer. Rita glanced over her shoulder. She looked at the models in front of her, then behind her. There was no mistaking that she was surrounded by a sea of stunningly beautiful women. Passersby stopped to ogle or to ask for the girls' phone numbers.

In the sun, Rita felt another oily bead of sweat roll down from her hair to her face. As she wiped off the sweat with her hand, she heard Annie-Marie cringe, "eww!"

Rita's confidence was waning. Just then, she caught sight of her reflection in the glass window straight ahead. Was she a model, really? Who was she kidding? On account of her accent, she even had trouble getting understood by the Americans. Would the modeling agency overlook this critical fact?

She looked down at her toenails.

"These toes have been through hell," she thought. She had put on two layers of red nail polish to conceal the cracks and stains, but she could still see right through the nail polish. Her toenails had been through hell; each one told a story—of the thorns that impaled them, of the rocks she crashed into as she played barefooted on the Kenyan plains. She studied her toenails again.

Chipped-toe!

The American who had mispronounced her second name (Cheptoo) as "chipped-toe" could have been right. Rita's chances at The Bleep Modelling Agency were getting slimmer.

All around her, she noticed that all the other aspiring models had perfectly pedicured toes. Rita was skinny, yes, but she lacked the boldness that the other models possessed. Her large behind attracted quite some stares back home. In her village she was considered to be one of the most beautiful women; men, old and young, tried to pursue her. The gap on her front teeth was a sign of beauty. Her father used to call her his princess. Even though, there were other black girls around, Rita seemed to be ten shades darker than the next darkest girl.

"No one had her kind of hair," she thought as she dug her fingers into her thick oily hair.

What was she thinking? Her heart began to pound. She felt tears swelling in her eyes. Should she stay and see what happens? She thought she had no chance at all.

She felt like a big failure, who had wasted her life on a pursuit she knew, deep down, to be a fantasy. She was clearly out of place.

Rita turned and began to walk away. Her sweat glands finally gave in, as multiple beads of sweat mixed with coconut oil came racing down her forehead and neck. This time she didn't bother wiping them off. She just wanted to get away as fast as she possibly could, from those models. Was she better off hiding in the sea of nurses? Was her father right after all? She knew she had to bury the child within and think of her future realistically. Her first step would be to return and secure her place again in college. *As she crossed the busy street, and missing being hit by the cars by inches, she had the urge to weep, but did not.

She looked up and saw a couple of men on a crane on a tall church building, who were unfolding a billboard banner. Out of curiosity, she stepped aside, eager to see what they were advertising. As they unfolded it, the writings popped out in bright red, and she curled her face in tears. Sniffling, Rita beheld the most beautiful love note she had ever seen:

"You are altogether beautiful, my love; there is no flaw in you." (Songs of Solomon 4:7)

Was this a message to her from the heavens? It had to be! It dawned on her that she didn't need to be told she was beautiful. She already knew. She was the apple in her father's eyes. Since she was a little girl, her father always called her his princess. The memory of such sweet moments of her infancy renewed Rita's confidence. She quickly wiped her tears and turned back toward Bleep Modeling Agency, her shoulders held high. She felt unshakeable.

The Rain Birds' Dilemma

The sky was clear. No clouds were in sight. High up on the pine trees, two green woodpeckers—the villagers called them rain birds—sang and chirped. In the bushy, branchy trees, the birds' green bodies could hardly be seen, but their crimson napes were clearly visible. They sang their hearts out, each taking turns to warn the villagers of the rain to come.

Outside her hut, Wanjiku sat watching the two rain birds. She was fascinated. Their songs and cackles mesmerized her. For as long as she could remember, the rain birds had never let down her community. They had always been accurate on the arrival of the rain. Already, she and her brothers had finished sowing the maize and bean seeds. How they longed for the rain!

Not far from where she sat, a group of late teen, girls in her age group, were huddled together. They were discussing the color of beads, earrings and wraps they would wear to the singles *Muchungwa* dance, to be held at sundown. Wanjiku remembered that, the previous year, she attended the dance, and vowed never, ever to attend any such dance again, she swore. What a waste of time the event had been!

Wanjiku's image of the singles dance was still fresh in her mind. She recalled how the men watched the girls like hawks. The young women in attendance sat over the bonfire, keenly aware of the men's stares. Even as they whispered among themselves, and pretended to be uninterested, they did everything in their power to get the men's' attention. They giggled, rolled their eyes and pouted their lips in an attempt to look ever more attractive. Wanjiku believed that women were queens and worthy of being pursued, and should, therefore, not behave in such helpless and desperate manner.

Clearly, something had to be wrong with the young women of her village. How could they be interested in the men or at a *Muchungwa* dance? Surely there was more to life! From her place outside her hut, Wanjiku shook her head, in astonishment *No thank you!* she thought. Despite her father's pleas that she attends the singles dance, she had no intention of going there, ever.

The previous night, her father had said to her, "Wanjiku, you need to go to *Muchungwa*. That's the only way you will get suitors. Or do you wish to die a maiden?"

Wanjiku did not care much for marriage. She had read a lot of storybooks on the subject. From her

English class, a story that stood out was *Cinderella*. It was her favorite. The love and adventure in the story were engrossing. What especially caught her attention about the love tales was that the men treated the women with passion and love. But not so in the village. In real life, Wanjiku only knew that the men would not go to such great lengths to court a woman. They rarely made their soft feelings known. She had never seen a man weep or display emotion, unless it was in anger. She had seen a man beat his wife in public over burned dinner or failure to answer promptly to his calls. Wanjiku longed to be wooed and loved like *Cinderella*.

In her thinking, marriage was a death sentence. Even as she had listened on many occasions as her father implored her to attend the singles dance, she could not help but wonder if there was a single man, apart from her father, who could truly love and respect his wife. Unlike most men, he respected her mother and his first wife. As far as Wanjiku knew, her father had never beaten or scolded her mother or his first wife.

Wanjiku's father was indeed an extraordinary man. It was no secret that he loved Wanjiku more than his other children. Wanjiku was the only girl and the last born, of her parents. She had three brothers and seven stepbrothers from her father's first wife. It was perhaps because she was his youngest child that Wanjiku's father loved her so much. Or was it because of her tough and stubborn but pleasant character? Whatever the case, the 17-year-old girl felt loved and respected—at least within her father's household.

Her father had accorded her so many favors. He was patient with her refusal to get a suitor, and even allowed her to enroll in the English class with her brothers. In their village, schooling, especially for girls, was unheard of; in fact, it was frowned upon. Wanjiku was proudly aware that she was the first— indeed the only—girl to attend the class.

More than once, she had heard the village elders advising her father: "Be strict on your daughter," they scolded him. "If you allow her to keep attending school, she will bring shame to the village."

Wanjiku's God, *Ngai*, was, however, on her side, because her father refused to heed the caution of the elders. She grew to love her English class and especially her teacher, Ms. Potter.

Fifteen years before, Ms. Potter left Britain and settled in Kikuyu village as a missionary. She lived a stone's throw away from Wanjiku's home. Within a few years of her arrival, the white woman overcame the language barrier, and could now speak fluent Kikuyu. She slowly earned the trust and love of the villagers.

As a show of their affection for her, the people of the village built Ms. Potter a mud hut. In spite of the color of her skin, she now lived like any other villager. Whenever she was indoors, smoke billowed from her grass-thatched roof. She ate what they ate, dressed and spoke like a Kikuyu. After a few years, she persuaded the elders to allow her to start a two-hour English class in the village, and they agreed.

Later in the week, Ms. Potter was excited because

she was expecting an important visitor from Britain, and so she informed the class that there would be no classes for the entire week. How bored and idle Wanjiku would be!

In addition to the missed English lesson, Wanjiku also learned to her dismay that her best friend, Wanjiru, would be unavailable for most of the week. Wanjiru would be busy discussing her attire with the other girls. Now Wanjiku would be truly bored. To keep herself busy and entertained, she decided to walk to the river and have a bath.

Her father had built a hut to be used by members of his household for baths. Wanjiku, however, preferred to take her baths in the river. She felt free there, and it was the most beautiful place she knew. Her favorite spot at the river was a secluded bushy area that was surrounded by tall jacaranda trees. Here, there was a beautiful bloom of blue flower. Whenever the sun shone, its rays passed through the flowers and reflected on the water, creating a bed of bouncing pattern of colors that Wanjiku thought were breathtaking.

Wanjiku drew closer to the river, she wore a yellow wrap that hugged her body and complemented her slim figure. At the river, she slowly took off her garment. She smiled, anticipating the cool water on her body. She took off her beaded necklace that covered her long neck. Next, she removed her four metal earrings. Oh, Wanjiku despised the earrings. She often complained that they were a little too heavy for her liking. But she had to wear them anyway, because her mother said she had to keep them on at all times.

According to her mother, all unmarried girls were required to wear the earrings to distinguish them from married women, and so, over the months, the earrings had become part of Wanjiku's wardrobe. As she eased off her earrings, her ears felt a great sense of relief. She placed the earrings, necklaces and wrap together on a rock. Then she eased herself into the river.

At first, the coolness of the water tickled her senses. She giggled with pleasure as the water cooled her body. Then, absent-mindedly, she began to sing the rain song that her mother used to sing to her since she was a baby.

Ũka bura ũka bura (Come rain, come rain)

Tũnyoni twina marũa, (The birds have a letter)

Marũa marauga bura ĩ njĩra (The letter says the rain is on the way)

Ũka bura ũkabura (Come rain, come rain)

Nĩkwambia na gũthuthua (It has started drizzling)

Irio ciheo maĩ. (To water the seeds on the ground)

Ũka bura ũka bura (Come rain come rain)

As she sang, her voice echoed back and forth between the jacaranda trees and the rocks in the river. She sang on, while flailing her arms and legs about in the shallow water with her eyes still closed.

When she opened her eyes, she was startled when she saw a man standing a few meters from the river, behind a tree. He stared right at her. Suddenly he turned and hastily walked away. His complexion was similar to that of Ms. Porter.

The water suddenly felt ice-cold and Wanjiku

began to shiver violently. She also became aware that her heartbeat had quickened. She was visibly shaken and for a few moments, she stood still in the water. "How dare him? Does he know it is a taboo to see an unmarried woman naked?" She thought angrily. She knew that respectable men, like her father, would never peek at a naked girl as she took her bath. She felt violated and at this point, she didn't know whether she should she get out or stay in the water? She wasn't so sure now. What if the stranger was still out there?

Unwilling to risk being watched again naked by the unfamiliar person, she ran and put on her wrap. She relaxed a little once her body was covered. With her necklaces and earrings back in place, she stood against the rays of the sun, hoping the sun would provide some heat. She was still dripping wet, her wrap clinging to her body. On any other day, she would have laid down on the grass and let the sun dry her before throwing on her wrap, *but not today. Her safe space had been compromised. Her safe haven wasn't safe anymore, after all.

As Wanjiku arrived at her village, one of the girls looked at the beads on Wanjiru's braided hair and said, "Wanjiru, large beads are not good for you. Try these small, red ones. They will make you look smaller."

The other girls giggled, looking Wanjiru over.

"Why? I have always worn large beads. I think they make me look good," Wanjiru said, not quite getting their point.

At this point, the rest of the girls were still in the group discussing their clothes choices, and so they did not notice Wanjiku's arrival, or that she looked unusually shaken. She entered her hut and did not get out until it was time to prepare dinner. By this time, her friend Wanjiru had worn her brand-new wrap. She had also fashioned a necklace from small beads and eagerly waited for the dance to start.

Wanjiru had always wanted to be married and to have children. Unlike Wanjiku, Wanjiru wanted a husband. She was plump and short and had freckles all over her face. Her neck was so short that she could only wear one necklace. She made up for this with four earrings in each ear. Wanjiru wore knee-high wraps that showed much of her legs.

Wanjiku looked at her friend and muttered under her breath, "What sheer desperation!" There was no doubt that Wanjiru was desperate for a husband.

Wanjiru once said to Wanjiku, "I would do anything to have your figure and that long neck. I have seen how the men stare at you."

"Wanjiru, there is more to life than men," Wanjiku responded. "Have you ever been curious about life outside this village? Have you ever wanted to experience something new?"

"Wanjiku, stop being a dreamer," Wanjiru countered. "You clearly know that there is only so much a woman can do. We were born and raised for marriage."

With that, Wanjiru hastily walked away.

As Wanjiku helped her mother prepare her father's dinner, she looked through the door of the hut, and noticed that the young women were assembling at the huge outdoors bonfire. The men had arrived before the ladies, and as each young woman arrived, she was examined for imperfections in dressing, personal beauty and the condition of her skin.

Wanjiku observed it all in dismay and muttered under her breath: "They inspect women like goats in the marketplace. And the women seem to like it!"

The women arrived one after the other, doing their best to make a good impression. Some overdid it. They either wore too much grease on their hair, or had on too many beads around their neck. To Wanjiku, they may well have been choking on their low expectations. What a waste!

Wanjiku's mother knew better than to ask her if she was going to the dance. They had had that discussion many times before and she knew Wanjiku's mind was made up.

"Wanjiku, if you don't get a suitor soon, we might need to find you one," her mother told her. "You are not getting any younger. If you remain stubborn, you may end up being a second wife to an old man. Keep that in mind."

Wanjiku remained sulky and restless as her mother spoke.

For a while, her mother was quiet. As they finished preparing dinner, the drums rented the air. From the corner of her eye, Wanjiku noticed that her peers were dancing. Some men faced the girls as they danced. Others jumped and hopped about the young women. In Wanjiku's thinking, it all looked sillier than it was entertaining. She knew for sure that all they would have to show for it were the sore muscles they would be nursing in the morning. Bored, she decided to call it a night.

In her room, she lay on her back, staring at the dry cheetah hide on her wall. The hide was one of her most treasured possessions. Her brother brought it home for her one evening as a gift, from a hunting expedition. The thought of him risking his life for her, made the item even more precious.

Just then, the image of the man she had encountered at the river came to her memory. For much of the day, even though she felt violated and angry, she had tried to brush the matter from her mind, but in vain. She visualized his skin complexion. It was different. *He looked a lot like Ms. Potter. Even the color of his eyes was different. Wanjiku had decided not to share her experiences at the river with anyone, including Wanjiru. It would be her little secret.

As she lay on her mat, deep in thought, she could still hear the drums, the songs and laughter outside. She was still visualizing the image of the man at the river when she drifted to sleep.

The following morning was slow. Her friends slept in longer than usual. When they finally woke up, they were achy and sluggish. By midday, Wanjiku had completed her chores. She had already fed and milked the cows. She had swept her father's compound.

When Wanjiru came over, Wanjiku noticed that her friend was in a bad mood. Throughout the morning, Wanjiru was sulky. Wanjiku knew why: no man had paid attention to her at the dance.

"Wanjiru, how was the dance?" Wanjiku asked as they gathered firewood at the fence.

"You should have come and found out for yourself," retorted Wanjiru.

Wanjiku had started to say something when, suddenly, Wanjiru announced that she was late with her chores. She stomped away, carrying her water pot with her, and avoided Wanjiku for the rest of the day.

Wanjiku *was free the rest of that day, and was wondering what she would do with her time between then and dinner? To keep herself occupied, she decided to pay Ms. Potter a visit. They had become close friends. Wanjiku loved to watch her British friend paint the landscapes.

Having grown up in this hilly village, Wanjiku found the endless hills and plains to be a boring sight. And the many shapeless mud huts didn't make the landscape any less unexciting. But when Ms. Potter put everything on canvas, it was like seeing it all from a different perspective. Ms. Potter had a way of working her magic around the most ordinary things.

Ms. Potter was sitting outside her hut, reading what looked like a letter. Something about the letter must have grabbed her complete attention because she did not see as Wanjiku approaching. When she finally looked up, Wanjiku saw tears in her eyes. Wanjiku had never seen her English teacher cry. Clearly, something was wrong.

"Ms. Potter, is anything the matter?" Wanjiku asked.

"Oh, I hate for you to see me like this," said Ms. Potter. "My nephew came and brought me this letter from my brother. I just realized that I miss him so much."

She used the back of her hand to wipe the tears from her eyes.

Wanjiku was at a loss for words. She had never been away from her family, so she didn't know how it would feel not see them. Often, she had the feeling that she saw too much of her family. Perhaps she could have benefited from a little space. But Ms. Potter was different. Wanjiku awkwardly put her arms around Ms. Potter and they sat in silence for a while.

Soon, they were distracted by a male voice just behind them. They both turned and Wanjiku held her breath. It was the same man she had encountered at the river! Wanjiku stared intently at him and she was uneasily aware that he too was staring right back at her.

After an awkward minute, Ms. Potter laughed nervously. Then, addressing the man, she said, "Eric, this is Wanjiku, my dear friend and student."

She turned to Wanjiku.

"And Wanjiku, meet my nephew, Eric. He is the visitor I was expecting from Britain. He is on vacation, and he decided to come and visit me for a month."

Wanjiku was too startled to utter a word. Without thinking, she rose to her feet and ran off as fast as she could. She needed to put as much distance as possible between herself and the white stranger, who had seen her completely naked.

She stopped, panting, when she finally got to the river. Already, her skin felt hot, as if she was running a fever. She sprayed some water on her face. She would have liked to have a full-body bath, but the image of the stranger staring again at her was overwhelming, so she decided against undressing or immersing herself in the water.

Sitting on a rock at the bank, she dipped her legs in the water and sat staring at her toes. She had not thought this through. Why did she run? What would be her next course of action? What would she tell Ms. Potter? Confused, she just sat there, staring into the water, at the little ripples that formed when she thrashed her feet and wiggled her toes.

When she looked up, Eric was sitting by her side. How did he get here? Had he sprinted after her?

Her heart skipped a beat. Again, his blue eyes stared straight into hers. She felt hypnotized and could not take her eyes off him.

"Don't be scared of me," Eric said with a deep,

foreign accent. "And please don't run."

Wanjiku was speechless. She wanted to run again but could not get herself to stand or move. She sat and listened to him.

"This place is prettier than where I come from. There is nothing better than fresh air. Back home, we have lots of tall buildings. But nothing beats the huts and the simplicity you have here," he said.

As he spoke, he brushed a strand of his tanned hair from his face.

Wanjiku did not say anything, so Eric continued, "I am trying to get used to all the walking. My aunt tells me it's what keeps all of you in such good shape."

Eric now stopped to inspect his toes, which he wiggled in the water. Then he said, "But all the walking takes some getting used to. Back home in Britain, I use the train. And I just bought a new car."

Still, Wanjiku did not comment. By now, her fear of Eric had begun to melt away. Soon, she found herself mumbling in response, nodding along and laughing nervously at his jokes.

At times, she never quite understood what he said. His accent was strange, and his manner of speaking was hurried, and his words and phrases appeared to be disjointed.

Was that how the British people spoke? Wanjiku wondered, realizing that Ms. Potter had a similar accent.

Of course, Eric's English was more complex than Ms. Potter's. Perhaps Ms. Potter chose to speak slower to make it easier for her students to understand. Still, Wanjiku understood most of what Eric said. Ms. Potter's English classes had been a great help. And then she loved to watch Eric talk.

He walked her home and promised to visit her the following day.

Eric made a point to see her every day, and Wanjiku slowly warmed up to him. He made her feel beautiful and important. He was unlike any other man she had met.

"Here in the village, the men spoke to the women as if they were superior. They are so rude," Wanjiku thought. Eric treated her as an equal. Each morning he helped her feed the cows and do her chores. And then he walked her to her English class in the afternoons.

Their friendship did not go unnoticed in her village. One afternoon she came home from her class to find the village elders waiting to speak to her. The old men did not make routine visits. They never made house calls. Wanjiku knew this fact well. Why, then, were the elders here?

"Wanjiku, we hear you have been busy," one of the elders said.

"What do you mean?" Wanjiku asked. She knew well what they were trying to say.

"That boy you have been seeing, aren't you ashamed?" the elder asked, then added, "It's taboo and, to make matters worse, he is a missionary. You know that our tribe doesn't allow that. It's completely improper."

Wanjiku swallowed hard.

Just then, the elder said abruptly, "Expect consequences, young girl!"

The other elders nodded their heads in agreement.

Wanjiku understood the consequences of breaking the rules of the Agikuyu. Was she willing to take that risk for Eric? She didn't want to let down her family. She especially did not wish to disappoint her father.

Not long thereafter, her father called her into his hut. After confronting her, he grabbed her by the arm and gave her a beating. She screamed and her mother had to come to her rescue.

In all her life, Wanjiku had never seen her father so outraged. He said he regretted giving her so much freedom. But that would change.

Days changed to weeks. As promised, Wanjiku lost her freedom and her friends too. Wanjiru avoided her altogether and her mother was stricter than usual. Wherever Wanjiku went, her mother now followed. Worse, her English class was forbidden. Her life was falling apart.

What would she do? She was torn between the feelings she now had for Eric and her loyalty to her tribe. Suddenly, she was confused. Why did she have to choose between Eric and her tribe? But she could have the two.

Even as she worried both for herself and for her British friend, Wanjiku, like the rest of the villagers, was concerned about the danger of drought. The rains had never been this late.

One evening, when everyone was asleep, Eric sneaked into Wanjiku's hut. They spoke for a moment, after which he left. This was risky, both for him and for Wanjiku. The village warriors were under orders to keep an eye out for him. Soon, the night visits became a habit. Every night, Eric tiptoed into the hut. After moments of talking in whispers, he would again sneak out as quietly as he had come.

One night, Eric said he was returning to Britain, because his father was ill. The thought of saying goodbye was too much for Wanjiku. He was her one true friend; she had come to love him very much.

Soon, she found herself thinking deeply about Cinderella. Wanjiku thought about the little girl's misfortunes, how Cinderella was mistreated by her stepmother and stepsisters. She thought about how Prince Charming would finally choose Cinderella in spite of her poverty, and their life of romance and happiness ever after.

Previously, Wanjiku had not believed in love. Slowly, it dawned on her that she was, in fact, Cinderella. True love and passion really did exist!

"Wanjiku, I love you," Eric said. "I will never forget you."

As he spoke, he choked with emotion.

"But why does it have to end like this, Eric?" Wanjiku asked as tears fell uncontrollably.

Eric put his arms around her and gave her a kiss— Wanjiku's first kiss. That closeness triggered feelings she did not even know she was capable of. They shared a night of passion filled with urgency and fire. She lay in his arms, holding on to him, never letting go.

Wanjiku felt like her heart was breaking when he left the following day. She thought of him every single day. Sometimes when she closed her eyes, she could still feel his close embrace and the tender kisses they had shared. Wanjiku longed for the day when she could see him again.

Days turned to months. One day, as Wanjiku peeped through a hole in her father's fence, she noticed that the earth was parched. The grass was all gone. The maize and bean seeds that they had sown months before had gone to waste. The rain birds had been wrong this time. There would be no rain after all. Unluckily, the rain birds had abandoned the land.

Wanjiku held her belly, where Eric's seed lay. She still felt angry and hurt. Angry that she had to go through this alone, angry at herself for being so naive, and letting her guard down. She should have chosen her family over him. He had been gone for four months, and she had not heard from him. A lot had happened since then.

Wanjiku went before the elders and sincerely apologized to them. Afterward, the elders agreed that even though she had made a grave mistake, she was a part of them, the community. After all, the Agikuyu tribe believed in peaceful resolutions, and strongly adhered to an old and famous proverb: *mwaki ndūhoragio na mwaki*—fire doesn't extinguish fire.

The elders agreed that she would be given a small piece of land outside her father's compound. She would till this land and provide for herself. This was necessary considering that she had refused to get married to a local, elderly man as his third wife.

After hearing the deliberations, Wanjiku remembered how her father had described to her the unity of the Agikuyu tribe. He said the Agikuyu were like the three stones that support a cooking pot on the fire: take away any one stone and the pot would collapse. As with the stones, among the Agikuyu each person depended on the others. They all believed in *Ūmūndū* (humanity), forgiveness and unity. "We are each other's keeper," he said. Carrying on, he stated, "When one person in down, it affects the whole tribe."

This explained why they didn't banish her.

Wanjiku peeped through her father's fence once more. She had a flashback to her youthful days...

Although Wanjku's relationship with her family was strained, her brothers and father helped her build a hut and a bed. She lived on food that was delivered every morning, wrapped in banana leaves, by a person she might never identify.

Ms. Potter was asked to leave, and at this point she was already back in Britain. The villagers blamed her, saying she was the cause of the greatest shame to ever befall the Kikuyu tribe.

When she was leaving, Wanjiku gave her a message to deliver to Eric. She would inform him that she was pregnant with his baby. Already, four months had passed without a word from him. Why was Eric silent? The men in her village might not be as romantic as Eric, but they sure knew how to take responsibility.

Wanjiku peeped through her father's fence once more, and had a flashback of her youthful days, when she would chase after her brothers in the lush, green grass of her father's compound. His compound now looked bare and lifeless.

She looked up to *Ngai*, tears streaming down her face, and prayed that he would forgive her and heal her people's land. As she walked back to her little, desolate hut, she felt a warm breeze. She was stunned because, for months, the air had been hot, almost unbearable. She looked up and saw a lonely cloud in the sky. It seemed to beckon the other clouds, which slowly moved in from all corners of the sky, merging into a huge, grey cloud. She stood in amazement. Just then, a drop fell. More drops followed. Soon, the heavens opened up.

Completely soaked, she raised her hands and fell on her knees in complete surrender. She could feel all the hate and resentfulness toward Eric, and the feelings of guilt that weighed her down, wash away. She felt renewed, as though she had been cleansed from the inside out. It was a divine moment.

The Hyena's
Last Laugh

The *laughter of the hungry hyenas were louder on this night than on any other night. In their pen, the cattle restlessly paced up and down, unable to ignore the looming danger. Isina, unable to sleep, turned and glanced at her only sister, who lay on the mat beside her. The moonlight seeped through the cracks of their mud hut and lit up her heart-shaped ebony face, making it glow in the dark. She looked so much at peace. Isina wished she could say the same for herself.

From their distance, the hyenas always eyed their cows, and Isina was used to their laughs. All her life, she had lived with them. The killers were harmless as long as the bonfire was kept on throughout the night and the warriors kept watch.

But Isina's biggest nightmare was about to unfold. At sunrise she would turn fourteen years old. Without a doubt, this was not a day of celebration. As she knew, every fourteen-year-old girl in the village had to face the knife. It was the customary passage to adulthood. Isina could almost feel the blade of the rusty knife cutting up her insides and taking away her freedom.

What a barbaric act! she thought. She had often heard the older girls speaking about their painful experience.

One girl said, "I bled so much I thought I would die."

Another girl reminisced, "That was the most

painful experience I have ever had to endure."

The thought of being stripped naked and getting forced down, her legs split wide open as someone cut her up, gave her the chills. Aware of the advancing night, she felt sorry for herself. Already, she was trembling. The thought of running away had crossed her mind, but where would she run to?

Her rural home, Longonot village, was located in the semi-arid land in southern Kenya, away from everyone else. The closest neighbors were fifty kilometers away, but they were at odds with her village. Because these neighbors were cattle rustlers, the people of Longonot feared and avoided them. In any case, if she decided to run away, she would have to walk for a long distance, barefoot, on the hot, sandy soil, under the scorching sun.

Isina prayed that *Enkai*, her God, would intervene. How she wished that time would stand still so that the sun would not rise!

From her hut, she could hear her father's loud snores. Why did the man snore so hard? Perhaps it was because of all the meat he ate. Each of his wives had a day to feed him. And each wife had her turn sharing the mat with him at night. Tonight, was her mother's turn.

Isina had considered telling her mother about her fears and asking her if there was a way out. She knew all too well the consequences of such disobedience. She and her mother would be cast out of the village. They would lose all they had, including their family and friends. She knew this because her aunt Namunyak, her mother's youngest sister, had run away from her planned circumcision when Isina was 8 years old. Many thought she would not make it out alive in the desolate land, and she was assumed dead. They thought she would die of starvation, if not fall prey to the hyenas.

Isina was especially sad to lose her, because they had grown very fond of each other. Their friendship began when Aunt Namunyak caught her setting free the fattened sacrificial goat from its pen. The animal was set to be sacrificed the following day. She laughed at Isina's look of shock but promised not to tell anyone. From that day, Namunyak told Isina that she saw a fire in her eyes, and that there was something different and special about her. At the time, Isina didn't understand what her aunt meant, and brushed it off as crazy talk. But it felt good that someone thought she was wonderfully different.

Five years after that incident, as Isina was untangling a trapped bird from the top of a baobab tree, which she considered her own, someone called out her name from under the tree. She almost fell off the tree when she realized it was her aunt, Namunyak. Isina's aunt looked completely different. She wore a flowery yellow dress and had combed her hair Afro style. They managed to talk for a few minutes before Isina was chased away by the village warriors, and warned never to return. Sadly, they didn't even allow her to say farewell to her mother or sisters. Namunyak got into a waiting car, and that was the last Isina saw of her.

Isina lay on her mat, deep in thought. She drifted

off to sleep late into the night, having made up her mind. She was awakened by the loud commotion outside her hut. Already, her sister was up: her mat had been rolled and leaned on the wall. Her heart pounding, Isina quickly rolled her mat and stepped outside. A crowd of villagers stood staring at cattle carcasses that had been killed by the hyenas.

Before the crowd stood the three warriors who had been on the night watch. The three, their spears still in hand, looked down in shame. Everyone knew the warriors had to have been asleep when the hyenas struck. The bonfire was also long dead, which meant the men forgot to add in firewood.

This had happened once before when Isina was ten. She knew the price the warriors would have to pay. They would have to find a way to pay back all the dead animals. For sure, the only way they could pay the penalty was by raiding their neighbors and stealing their cattle.

While this was bad news for the village, Isina knew it was the perfect distraction she needed. Might they forget all about her looming birthday celebration? Among the people in the crowd was her father; he too had lost a few of his cows. For a moment, the man appeared lost in thought. Then, slowly, he turned from the crowd and walked toward Isina.

"Happy birthday, Isina. Your big day is finally here," he said.

"Yes Baba," she whispered.

Isina's father, with his protruding belly, had always vented his anger on his twelve children and his wives. He was a hot-tempered man and his family knew to keep away from him, especially on such days.

The memory of her stepsister's celebration was still fresh in her mind. Isina remembered that her sister had pleaded with her father to save her from the ritual. All that the girl had succeeded to obtain from the man was a beating. After that, she did not speak to anyone for months.

Aware of her impending suffering, Isina excused herself and went to help her mother prepare breakfast. After she finished her chores—fetching

drinking water from the well and feeding the calves—
*Isina enjoyed to pass time on her baobab tree, also
called the tree of life. Her tree of choice was huge and
stood taller than all the other trees in the village. It
was one of a kind. The villages used its bark for
medicine and ate its fruit. Its umbrella-like branches
were strong enough to support her lightweight body
and she knew how to maneuver her way to the top.
From this point, she could see miles away. Many
times, her father had caught her in the tree, and he
had cautioned her against it. Once, he gave her a
beating for disregarding his warning to stay away
from the tree. In spite of the admonition, Isina always
found her way to her baobab tree.

As Isina sat upon the highest branch, she
wondered what was beyond the horizon. She longed
to travel, to see the world and meet new people. But
she kept these thoughts to herself. If her father ever
got wind of her rebelliousness, he would marry her
off.

Isina's father was a traditional man who disliked

complications. Once, she overheard him saying that the outside world was for men only. A woman's place, he said, was at home. A woman's duty was to meet the needs of her husband and children.

Her celebration wasn't until midday. As she sat up on her tree, she couldn't help but wish. She wished she could see the heavy dust of an approaching car. Maybe the strange-looking missionaries, who came into Longonot village every week, would drop by today.

No adult paid the missionaries much heed. But the children loved and treasured them. With their every visit, they brought sugary treats that were wrapped in colorful paper. The children loved them. Of course, first, the children had to agree to sit and listen to the missionaries' stories, which Isina found fascinating. The missionaries talked about a far-away land, a place where people lived, talked and dressed differently. The missionaries' god lived up beyond the clouds. It was a far-fetched story, but interesting, nevertheless.

"Isina, come down from that tree this instant," her mother called out, rudely interrupting her thoughts.

"Yes mama," she said as she hurried down.

"Your father has warned you about that tree. It's time for your celebration. I will be the one taking you."

Isina's mother, seeing her hesitation, grabbed her hand and dragged her to the house of her father's sister. The hut was stuffy and smelled of dried herbs and fresh cow dung. Isina's aunt was a heavily built, gigantic woman. Babies cried at the sight of her. Isina had never seen her smile or speak a polite word to anyone. It was rumored that the reason her husband had left her for a younger woman was because she was barren.

Isina's aunt probably chose this line of work because she was a bitter human being who needed to inflict pain on others. Her satisfaction seemed to come from heartlessly making young girls scream and taking what was precious from them.

The woman had readied everything she would need. There was a sharp, glaring knife on a little table. Also, at hand was a sheep skin to lie on, herb water to wash the wound and cow fat to seal it up.

Isina could hardly breathe. Cold sweat welled up at the back of her neck and streamed down her spine. What if she bled to death?

She went over her plan one more time. What if everything backfired? Time was running out. Where were they?

Then it happened. The car finally arrived. She could hear them honking, as always to attract the villagers' attention.

Isina pushed her mother aside and bolted out of the hut. She ran as fast as her feet could carry her toward the car and held on tightly to the first missionary who got off the car.

This missionary was a young woman with long, jet-black hair. She wore a black T-shirt, green cargo pants and brown boots. On her neck was a gold necklace that bore a huge cross.

Isina tried to tell her what was going on, but the missionary did not seem to understand. Luckily, the missionaries had brought with them a translator, who explained everything. As she listened, the female missionary was visibly shocked.

Looking in the direction of Isina's home, where her mother and aunt stood, staring in disbelief, the missionary put a protective arm around the girl. Isina's heart almost stopped when she saw her father coming. She clung even harder onto the missionary.

"Isina, what is all the commotion about?" he asked her.

She did not respond.

Isina's aunt, who had approached, replied, "She refuses to face the knife."

"What? You coward! You will do as I say."

The potbellied man advanced threateningly, but the missionary positioned herself between Isina and her father.

Understanding the commotion, the village warriors stood ready to attack.

Sensing that Longonot had turned hostile, the missionaries knew they were outnumbered. Their only chance was to flee. Quickly, they boarded the car and drove away, taking Isina with them.

"Stop them! You thieves!" Isina's father shouted after the speeding vehicle.

As the car drove off, Isina heard her father's final warning: "Isina, if you do not come back here at once, I will disown you. You will no longer be my daughter."

His outburst died down, drowned off by the increasing distance and the noise of the wheels on the rough road.

Behind the car, running after them, flailing her little arms while weeping and calling, was Isina's little sister. How sad Isina felt to realize that she was leaving her family behind! One day, she vowed, she would be back for her. She would return when it was safe. She would see her family again.

Behind the car, running after them, flailing her little arms while weeping and calling, was Isina's little sister.

As she was taken away by the missionaries, tears ran down her face. She felt relief and uncertainty— relief to have escaped her aunt's knife, and uncertainty about what the future held in store for her. Her deep prayer was that Aunt Namunyak was still where she had told her she would be if she needed her. Her aunt's information was still intact in her memory.

As the car hit the dirt road, she was sure she had heard the laughter of the hyenas in the nearby bushes. Their bellies were full of the heaps of meat acquired from the many cows they had killed in Isina's home village.

They all sat in the car in complete silence, deep in thought. Isina's heart was thumping hard, her hands clammy with sweat. She sat huddled close to the car door, shivering intensely, looking out of the window. The missionary kept looking at her, probably wondering where to take her. The translator, who sat by Isina, looked torn and confused. Drenched in sweat, the driver focused on driving as fast as he could. Perhaps he feared the warriors from the village were in pursuit.

After what felt to Isina like an eternity, they arrived at the town center. Isina looked around, then suddenly asked if they could stop immediately, because she needed to use the bathroom. The driver stopped. Isina quickly opened the door and sprinted out, running as fast as she could toward the store, which was written in bold capital letters—"Namunyak Clothes Store." Isina ran straight into her aunt's open arms.

The Illicit Storm

The gray clouds raced across the sky and appeared to converge right above the spot where Wacuka stood on the vacant school grounds. She half ran and half walked, trying to avoid the sharp glaring eye of the storm that was threatening to encompass her. As the light of day turned gray, the wind gathered momentum. Wacuka watched the tall cypress trees blowing this way and that, their heavy branches creaking in what was about to become a tempest.

All around her, dust swirled, and forced her dress to waltz to an awkward *Mwomboko* dance. She had to shield her eyes from the flying grains of dirt. When a second gust of wind blew, she clung to her dress but not before the garment was pushed up to her midriff.

Wacuka could feel her cheeks burning with embarrassment, and her heart thumping hard in her chest. In her rush to get to school that morning she had not paid any particular attention to her undergarments. She quickly held down her dress, and then looked around, hoping no one had seen the wind's invasion of her privacy. She breathed out in relief when she realized there was no one in sight. She would not be repeating that mistake.

Wacuka had a long way to go before she got home to the famous Witeithie village, which was located at the heart of Kihubuini sub-location in central Kenya. Her school, Kihubuini Secondary School, was approximately 2.4 kilometers from the village. To get

All around her, dust swirled, and forced her dress to waltz to an awkward *Mwomboko* dance.

home, she would have to go over a hill and cross over the narrow Nihaku River.

She wished she had left school immediately after the classes ended, instead of whiling away the hours under the *Mugumo* tree with her best friend, Wangechi, watching the boys playing soccer. Both Wacuka and Wangechi knew they had no interest in the game. They only stayed behind to watch the boys' shirtless upper bodies, as the boys ran about chasing the ball and shouting at each other.

Wacuka had a particular liking for Kimathi, the tall, dark, handsome school Head Boy and soccer captain. Kimathi was the son of Mzee Njuguna, who was also the chief of Kihubuini village. Rumor had it that, after high school, Kimathi hoped to join the University of Nairobi to study medicine. The boy walked with authority and boldness, and always left a trail of girls drooling after him.

On many occasions, Wacuka had deliberately drifted in his direction, as if by accident, hoping to catch his attention. Sadly, she never won as much as a glance from him. Although Wacuka realized the boy was out of her league, she was not discouraged.

After the game of soccer that day, she found herself all alone. Wangechi, whose home was situated a few meters from the school, only gave excuses as to why she could not escort her. That day, she said she had chores to do before her parents came home.

As Wacuka began walking home, the rain fell, softly at first. As a drop rolled down her bony cheek, she hoped the expected storm would never come. Soon, however, the raindrops intensified. Within a matter of minutes, the skies really opened up, and now Wacuka was in real trouble. The now heavy downpour formed a dense curtain that made it impossible for her to see ahead. Luckily, she had taken this path numerous times; she could find her way home blindfolded.

The weight of her soaking school bag was getting increasingly unbearable on her back. There was no telling what condition her books, especially her absorbent notebooks, were now in. She always kept them clean and neat, and used an ink pen to take down her class notes. Already, she could visualize the smudges that the ink and the rain had formed.

Thoughts of taking refuge under a leafy jacaranda tree crossed her mind. But she knew the story of Mzee Jacob's tragic death only too well. Mzee Jacob was one of her father's drinking buddies. After searching for him all night, his wife found his dead body, leaned against a tree, early one morning. His skin had turned blue-black. Everyone said a jolt of lightning had caused it. Apparently, Mzee Jacob had been struck the night before, on his way home from his daily escapades of drinking *muratina*, the local brew.

At that early hour, his wife's screams attracted a huge crowd. Wacuka's mother, who had been home when her husband's body was brought in by mourning villagers, used the incident to warn Wacuka and her brother against shielding themselves from the rain under a tree. She also cautioned about the consequences of *muratina*, which she said had ruined the lives of many village men in Kihubuini.

According to Mama Wacuka, a drunken man with a belly filled with *muratina*, sitting under a tree in a thunderstorm, was the perfect recipe for disaster. She often reminded her children that had Mzee Jacob been sober, he would have seen the folly of standing under a tree on a stormy day.

Wacuka's knee-length blue tunic was now soaking wet and clung to her clammy body. She had planned to wear the same piece of school uniform again the next day but, by the look of things, she would have to wash and dry it as soon as she got home. Her shoes got heavier with the water and mud that clung to their soles. Already, the mud was sipping in through the holes in the shoes and ruining her socks. This pair of shoes had served her well for the four years she had been in high school. Her father, who was referred to as Baba Wacuka in the village, always said it was a waste of money to buy new shoes when the old ones could be repaired. She was glad that, in another two weeks, she would sit for her final exam and would discard them immediately thereafter.

Every time Wacuka's shoes developed a crack or a tear, she was advised to take them to the village cobbler, who charged five shillings per patch. By now, the shoes had several patches. Of course, she understood her father's reason for not buying her a new pair. He was an underpaid clerk, based at the local chief's office. He had worked there for as long as she could remember.

One day as Wacuka was cleaning her parents' room, she stumbled upon his school documents. He was a holder of a university degree in business administration, acquired from the University of Nairobi years before. The document was hidden in a metal box, kept under the old man's bed. *Why couldn't he find a better job, considering that he was an educated man?* she wondered. She kept her discovery a secret, for she did not wish to embarrass her father.

Baba Wacuka drank from Friday evening to Sunday evening, and was sober for the remainder of the week. Every Friday after work, he headed straight for the village bar, a wooden shack with a rusty roof, to drink *muratina*. The bar was a gathering of all types of village men—teachers, office workers, police officers, casual workers and shabby village idlers.

The *muratina* joint, an old, corroded place, was owned by Mama Kegi, who was named after the brown plastic kegs from which she served her drink, which she personally brewed. Mama Kegi was a plum, short woman, who had a deep masculine voice. She always wore a colorful headscarf, a revealing shirt, and flat sandals. She was considered an enemy by the village women, who thought of her as the devil who had stolen their husbands. Mama Kegi didn't seem to mind them. She preferred to keep to herself. Considering her many faithful clients, she had a constant flow of cash. What puzzled many, though, was that no matter how much she made, Mama Kegi did not seem to get any richer. She did not expand her business. She did not develop herself financially.

Because Mama Kegi's bar was not situated far from Wacuka's home, she usually heard the drunken men singing, often in unison, to popular tunes, including gospel songs. Unavoidably, at some point the intoxicated men would start a fight, and Mama Kegi would send them home.

Upon arriving home, often late at night and in a foul mood, Wacuka's father would demand to have his dinner served hot. Many times, the drunken man asked Mama Wacuka to wake up both Wacuka and Kamau, to keep him company as he ate. By now, they were all accustomed to this behavior, and knew never to argue with him or there would be hell to pay.

As he slurped down his food, the man would reiterate his undying love for them, sometimes in the midst of tears. He would slur on about trivia that they often ignored, then at the end of it all, he would remind them of the one indisputable fact—he was *Njamba ya mucii ũyũ* (the unquestionable head of the household). Satisfied, he would allow the children to go to sleep, but Mama Wacuka was always the last to go to bed. Every time, she stayed up until her husband collapsed on his chair and would drag him to bed.

"*Njamba ninii?*" (I am the man), she once heard her mother say under her breath as she dragged him to bed.

Wacuka was now navigating the sharpest peak of the hill. She could feel water streaming down from her heavy book-bag to her back. By this time, her shoes were nearly impossible to lift off the sticky ground. With every lift of her foot, she could feel that the soles were splitting off from their uppers. Once, she thought she heard threads snapping loose. There was no doubt that her shoes had come to the end of their life.

She bent and took off her shoes and socks. Both had browned from the thick paste that the water and loam soil had made. In all her life she had never seen it rain this hard. Kihubuini had gone for a long time without rain. Why did this weather have to make this sudden entrance?

Wacuka paused to gaze at a tributary she knew well. Already, water flowed violently down this trail to the Nihaku River, which was more swollen now than ever. Could she safely cross Nihaku? She recalled when she was younger, she and other girls loved it here when it rained. How they had enjoyed sliding downhill on the mud! Today, however, the path was treacherous, perhaps even dangerous. But she had no other way of getting home. Taking a deep breath, she immersed one careful foot into the fast-flowing water. She felt the powerful current pulling her away and had to yank it out quickly.

Still, she was out of options. This was the only way. Mustering all her courage, she slowly inserted her right leg in, bracing for the worst, and then her left leg. There was no turning back now. Luckily, she did not slip or get dragged away. Still, she had to resist the powerful flow as she trudged along. She made it to the middle of the hill, but the descent turned out to be trickier than the ascent. Just when she thought she had a solid footing; she lost her grip and fell heavily in the mud.

Her body bobbed up and down in the water as it was dragged roughly down the river. "*Ngai,*" she screamed, hoping that God might hear her. As she was thrown about, she felt a sharp pain in her side. But she did not have much time to worry about the scrapes from rocks and branches floating about in the water. She was finally deposited by the mucky, violent waters—headfirst—into the Nihaku River.

Her entire body was now in pain. Nihaku was easily too deep for her and she tried to stay afloat. Her backpack was too heavy, and she would surely drown if she clung to the clammy package. Unwillingly, she let go of her bag. She was thrashing about, trying to stay alive, when she thought she heard a loud splash nearby. Just then, a pair of strong hands got hold of her and carried her across the river.

Initially, she had trouble telling who her savior was, because the person's full body was covered in mud and wet grass. Her rescuer scooped water in his hands and washed away the muck from his face. It was Kimathi, the handsome Head Boy of her school—son to Mzee Njuguna, the chief of Kihubuini.

Kimathi stood beside her, dripping water and panting. Wacuka was as confused as she was embarrassed. Kimathi looked her over and handed her soaked muddy bag to her. He walked away without uttering a word.

For a long time, wacuka just sat, out of breath, on a rock, thinking both of her ordeal in the raging water and mainly about her salvation by Kimathi. What a coincidence! It didn't feel real. She had day-dreamed about him for a long time, and almost concluded that he was out of her reach. What did all this mean? Did fate bring them together for a reason? *Maybe we will be classmates at the University of Nairobi someday,* she thought with a smile. All seemed possible now.

Still smiling, she rose and, not bothered by the fact that she had lost her shoes, or that many of her books were ruined, she picked up her soggy bag and lumbered through the mud and walked on home.

Six months later, Wacuka sat on the same rock by River Nihaku, clutching her admission letter to the University of Nairobi, where she would be studying law. She was ecstatic. She had emerged one of the top ten students at her school that had done well in the final examination. Her father was overwhelmed when he received her admission letter. He had bragged to all his beer buddies and bought a round of *muratina* for all of them in celebration.

She watched as the water in the river flowed slowly and leisurely—nothing compared to the day of the biggest storm in Kihubuini. A lot had happened since then. Even though she was extremely shy of Kimathi at school, she felt like she was at a better place with him. She could barely look him in the eye. Any time they met, she whispered a quick hello and rushed right past him. Her friend Wangechi had mentioned that Kimathi had also done well. Like her, he had been admitted to the University of Nairobi.

Wacuka moved closer to the edge of the rock and stood up. She could clearly see her reflection in the river. Holding her hand high, she shouted, "I promise to uphold the law and ensure justice for all, so help me God."

As she spoke, tears of joy streamed down her cheeks into the waters of the Nihaku River.

The Sacred Seeds

Nyakio knelt down, a look of sadness in her eyes. She held the red soil in her tiny, wrinkled hand and shook her head. Inhaling in despair, she dug her hand deep into the soil and took out a small shrunken potato. This was one of the many she had planted on her five-acres land on the plains of Matuhu in Murang'a, in central Kenya. She crushed the potato between her fingers and held them close to her nose, and deeply inhaled. She hoped she could smell something that would give her hope or indicate life. Disappointed, she tossed the bits of dry potato up in the air, and let the wind disperse them. The rains had failed her this year. Not once in her 50 years of life had she seen a drought so severe.

The wind blew, slowly at first, and then gradually intensified. Nyakio watched as the wind enticed the soil to a tango. Slowly, they danced from the ground up, twirling, entangled. The fierce wind encircled her and she had to cover her eyes. Her long flowery dress was blown about. A tear fell from her eye. She wasn't sure if it was caused by the dust in her eyes or by the feelings of sorrow. Were the soil and wind mocking her?

Nyakio recalled how successful the potato farm had been when her parents were still alive, and how, once, they harvested the biggest and healthiest potatoes in the land. Her parents had been the sole potato suppliers of a supermarket in the neighboring Thika Town.

For a while after her parents' demise, the farm did well. But the drought this year hit her really hard. She had seen tough times, but never anything this bad. Her father dug a small well for the household needs, but she wasn't sure it was enough to irrigate her five acres. The old man left clear instructions that the farm's ownership would fall under her care after he and his wife were gone. Following the death of the elderly couple after a battle with pneumonia eight years before, Nyakio became the owner of the farm.

At the time, in 1995, it was uncharacteristic for women to inherit land. This cultural practice was gradually changing. Before then, land could only be inherited by men. Women were expected to marry and cultivate their husband's land. From his deathbed, Nyakio's father had summoned his three brothers and the chief, and made clear his wishes: to leave his potato farm to Nyakio. His sons would have the rest of his properties.

This came as a surprise to Nyakio's two greedy brothers. The old man knew that Nyakio was the only one of his three children who had passion and love for his potato farm. Even while he was alive, Nyakio loved the farm. She had given up her college education and dedicated her life to potato farming. She had worked faithfully over the decades, by his side. She asked him questions, and she imitated whatever he did.

Soon, it became obvious that she was his favorite child. When they learned of their father's favor for Nyakio, they were visibly resentful. But when they discovered that their father was leaving the large farm solely to Nyakio, even before his death, their resentment turned to rage. The brothers went as far as calling Nyakio a witch. How had she managed to win over their father?

The brothers tried every tactic to convince her to give up the land. They even incited the farm workers to abandon her, but the workers remained loyal to her. The brothers made numerous attempts to sabotage her, but her faithful workers reported all their plans to her. Finally, the brothers approached

Nyakio's rich neighbor, Mzee Gitoro, and advised him to buy off their sister's land. Mzee Gitoro did everything to intimidate Nyakio into selling her property. Still, she did not budge.

Frustrated, the brothers moved away with the cattle, but not before demolishing her house and taking away whatever property was in it. Without shelter, Nyakio had to build herself a little wooden shed, vowing that once her farm made her a good profit, she would build a bigger, better brick house. Over the years, she remained in the shed.

Week after week, she waited for the rains. With every sunrise, she hoped that a miracle would befall her and the heavens would open up. She would visualize rain, the ground getting soggy, the appearance of tender shoots of the potatoes and, finally, a plentiful harvest. All this remained a fantasy. Was God angry with her? This could not be because, when she looked around her, she realized that everyone else was struggling. Eventually, she let go of her loyal workers for, she could not afford to pay them anymore.

She was saddened: some of the workers had been at the farm since the days of her parents and were like family. Sustaining herself during the famine was hard. She got by with the little money left after the sale of the last batch of potatoes still in the granary. Standing on her five-acre farm, her little shed and granary looked desolate in her desert-like farm.

One morning as she was throwing out dirty dish water at the side of her house, she noticed the strangest thing: some four little shoots were sprouting here. *But what plant was this?* she wondered. A neighbor passed by. Spotting the shoots, he informed her that the plant was unmistakably watermelon.

Then she remembered: when he had stopped by and tried to force her to sell her land to him, Mzee Gitoro, the rich village man, was munching on a piece of watermelon.

But he did not swallow the seeds; with every mouthful of the succulent fruit, he spat out the seeds. Watermelon was a fruit that only the wealthy could afford. Many times, Nyakio had seen the fruit at the market. As much as she had desired to taste it, she could not afford its price.

She vividly recalled the unsanitary eating habits of the rich man. With every mouthful, Mzee Gitoro would let the water out through the edges of his mouth, spitting out the seeds with little squirting sounds. It was the ugliest, most gluttonous sound Nyakio had ever heard. After discarding the peel at her doorstep, Mzee Gitoro wiped his wet hands on the pants of his green checked suit. Then he extended his hand to greet Nyakio.

"Mzee Gitoro, how may I help you?" she asked as she picked up her shrub-broom and began to sweep her small sitting room, one of the two rooms of her house.

"You know what I want. Let me take this burden off of your hands. Clearly you're in over your head."

"Mzee, my father entrusted me with this land. I'm sorry but I have to refuse your request."

With every mouthful, Mzee Gitoro would let the water out of his mouth, spitting out the seeds with little squirting sounds.

"You are a stubborn old woman," he said. "You will die an old spinster in this old shanty. Then I will take your land. Why not make some money from it while you are still alive?"

He turned to leave, then added, "Be wise: I can pay for the land now or take it for free when you die. It's your choice. You know where to find me," he said as he got into his old black Peugeot and sped away, leaving a cloud of dust.

Nyakio recalled how he would drive fast for some meters, then he would appear to have changed his mind. With a loud screeching of the breaks, he would back up his car, returning to the place closest to her house. She stood mortified when he suddenly began to drive back and forth, letting the wheels of his car make deep trenches on her rows of potatoes. She could see him wiping off the sweat from his brow, as if the gruesome act took him great effort. Then he drove to the entrance of her farm and disappeared.

How discourteous!

Every time she was on the verge of despair, she

reminded herself of the wisdom in a Kikuyu proverb that her father liked to share: *"Ciakorire Wacũ mũgũnda"* ("the fortunes from the heavens found Wacu busy in her farm"). Nyakio clearly understood that the proverb applied to her too—but she had to persist in working on her farm, if she were to profit from the good fortunes from above.

My hard work and perseverance will pay off someday, she consoled herself.

Every time she repeated the proverb to herself, a cloud of optimism would come over her, at least for a while. She could not give up now. She had given her word to her father that she would take care of the farm. She would remain true to her promise.

After about a month, the shoots' leaves had grown so big that they looked like they might choke each other out. The four plants needed transplanting. With careful hands, Nyakio uprooted the watermelon seedlings and transferred them to one of the rows on the potato farm. Although she doubted that they would thrive in the intense drought, she watered them every evening as the scorching sun went down.

A week later, they were flourishing. Two months later, each plant had four large fruits. Nyakio could hardly contain herself. After harvesting, she split open the fruits, took their seeds and planted them on other potato rows. The dead matter of the potatoes became useful after all. It now served as manure for the watermelon plants. Within three months, she harvested many more watermelons. This time, she was able to sell some at the local market. She scooped the seeds from a selected batch and planted them.

Late one night as she lay in bed, she thought she heard the sound of someone or something tapping on her tin roof. She listened, a little dazed, a little afraid. Then it occurred to her: it was the sound of little raindrops on her roof. Nyakio quickly sat up on her bed and rubbed her eyes. It was unmistakably rain! She jumped off her bed and opened her door. A gust of dusty wind greeted her. It would be followed by a heavy downpour.

In spite of the heavy downpour, she confidently

stepped out. She walked further out, mesmerized by the earthy smell produced when the rainwater hit the soil. She was quickly getting soaked and her nightdress *now clung to her skin. She should have sought shelter, but she did not need shelter. Rain was her friend. It felt like the hug of a long-lost friend.

In the darkness, she laughed out loudly, her hands stretched out into the sky. She danced her heart out. The feel of the mud between her toes was like the lather of soap on skin after a hard day. She cried—tears of joy—and let the tears blend with the rainwater on her face.

Nyakio's heart overflowed with gratitude both to her father and to her God. Her watermelons had multiplied. True to her father's words *"Ciakorire Wacŭ mŭgŭnda"*—the heavens had rewarded her hard work and perseverance.

Where was Mzee Gitoro? Was he even aware of the fortunes his aggression had generated? He paid her a hostile visit. He spat his seeds of discord at her, and she used these to erect a firm foundation of a watermelon estate. Surely, her God had not abandoned her.

Poem: I Am, Mama Africa

Arrows:
fall to her right
fall to her left
Others
Break on hitting her back
Crumbling as they hit the ground
But none
None touches her quiver.
This Quiver,
She guards with her life.

Her back
Scarred back now tough as steel.
Her sharp mind,
molded by divine wisdom
Her heart
Like a gentle kiss, from the sun's
first ray on the morning dew.
Her body speaks resilience
Courage
Grace.
Her eyes
Fiery eyes reflect strength
Radiate determination.

She sways her hips as she walks.
To the top of the hill
Even when all is not in place
She stands
Majestically
One hand on the waist,
The other on her stomach,
where lies her quiver.
With a thunderous voice,
she proclaims:
I am, Mama Africa.